# Uncle Pirate

Book by
**Ben H. Winters**

Music and Lyrics by
**Drew Fornarola**

Based on the Book *Uncle Pirate* by
Doug Rees

A SAMUEL FRENCH ACTING EDITION

# SAMUEL FRENCH

FOUNDED 1830

NEW YORK HOLLYWOOD LONDON TORONTO

SAMUELFRENCH.COM

## RENTAL MATERIALS

An orchestration consisting of a **Vocal** and **Piano/Vocal Score** will be loaned two months prior to the production ONLY on the receipt of the Licensing Fee quoted for all performances, the rental fee and a refundable deposit.

Please contact Samuel French for perusal of the music materials as well as a performance license application.

## IMPORTANT BILLING AND CREDIT REQUIREMENTS

All producers of *UNCLE PIRATE must* give credit to the Authors of the Play in all programs distributed in connection with performances of the Play, and in all instances in which the title of the Play appears for the purposes of advertising, publicizing or otherwise exploiting the Play and/or a production. The name of the Authors *must* appear on a separate line on which no other name appears, immediately following the title and *must* appear in size of type not less than fifty percent of the size of the title type.

In addition the following credit *must* be given in all programs and publicity information distributed in association with this piece:

**UNCLE PIRATE**
**Book by Ben H. Winters**
**Music and Lyrics by Drew Fornarola**
**Based on the book "Uncle Pirate" by Douglas Rees**

*UNCLE PIRATE* was first presented by Vital Theatre Company at Vital Children's Theatre in New York City, opening on January 16, 2010. It was directed by Jeremy Dobrish. The musical direction was by Julie McBride. The scenery was designed by Alexis Distler, with costumes by Bobby Pearce. The lighting was designed by Michael Gottlieb. Choreography was by Christine O'Grady. The production stage manager was Nicholas Rainey. The cast was as follows:

**WILSON**. . . . . . . . . . . . . . . . . . . . . . . . . . . . . . . . . . . . . .Steve Trzaska

**UNCLE PIRATE**. . . . . . . . . . . . . . . . . . . . . . . . . . . . . . . Joshua Nicholson

**CAPTAIN JACK** . . . . . . . . . . . . . . . . . . . . . . . . . . . . . . Amanda Yachechak

**WOMAN 1 (MOM, CARLA, ETC.)** . . . . . . . . . . . . . . . . . . . . . . .Beth Kuhn

**WOMAN 2 (MISS QUERN, ETC.)** . . . . . . . . . . . . . . . . . . . . . .Lauren Kampf

**MAN (DAD, PRINCIPAL PURVIS, ETC.)** . . . . . . . . . . . . . . . . .Ronn Burton

# CHARACTERS

**WILSON** – a nervous eight year-old with glasses. Very smart, very kind, very scared of the world.

**UNCLE PIRATE** – a tough-talking, barrel-chested, sword-rattlin', sea-garglin' old salt. Eye patch optional, heart of gold required.

**CAPTAIN JACK** – a wise-cracking penguin; played by an actor in a penguin suit

**WOMAN 1** (**MOM, CARLA**, various pirates and kids); Mom is the sensible long-suffering mother of Wilson; Carla is a bullying eight year-old with pigtails and a perpetual scowl.

**WOMAN 2** (**MISS QUERN**, various pirates and kids); Miss Quern is a secretary who looks and acts like a librarian – prim and proper, hair in a bun, etc.

**MAN** (**DAD, PRINCIPAL PURVIS, MR. TWISSEL**, various pirates and kids); Dad is the sensible long-suffering father of Wilson; Principal Purvis is a shifty-eyed middle-aged man whose great love is making life hard for children – later he is revealed to be a pirate. Mr. Twissel is terrified of everything, especially fourth graders.

**Scene One**

**At Very Elementary School**

*(An empty school yard. A kid runs on, ducks behind the basketball hoop [or a bush]. Slowly peeks out, takes a deep breath, and looks directly at the audience.)*

**WILSON.** Oh. Hi. I'm Wilson. You might be asking yourself, What is he doing? Great question. I'm hiding. What am I hiding from? Great question. Oh, you know. *Everything.* But, I mean, just for starters.

*(Enter mean, tough, **CARLA CANOVA**.)*

**CARLA.** I know you're here somewhere, Wilson. I smell wimp!

**WILSON.** *(sings)*
CARLA IS ALWAYS MEAN TO ME
IT'S LIKE SHE IS A MAC AND I'M A PC
SHE LIKES TO BREAK MY GLASSES
AND MAKE ME FEEL AFRAID
WHENEVER SHE'S CLOSE I SAY MY PRAYERS
AND QUIETLY TELL MYSELF THAT THERE'S
ONLY ONE HUNDRED FIFTY SIX DAYS
TILL I'M DONE WITH FOURTH GRADE.

**CARLA.** Alright, hand 'em over, squirt.

*(He hands over his eyeglasses.)*

**WILSON.** Can't you break someone else's glasses for a change?

**CARLA.** Let me think it over. But while I think it over, I'll break your glasses.

*(She bends his glasses and hands them back as the bell rings.)*

*(***WILSON**, **CARLA**, *and* **KID 2**, *now in a classroom, sit down. Enter* **MR. TWISSEL**, *frantic and wild-eyed, waving his chalkboard pointer.)*

**WILSON.**

MY TEACHER HAS GONE OUT OF HIS MIND
WHEN YOU TALK ABOUT BAD, NO CHILD'S LEFT BEHIND
I TRY TO JUST SURVIVE IT
AND IT MAKES ME SO AFRAID.
WHENEVER I'M IN THIS AWFUL CLASS
I PRACTICALLY BEG THE TIME TO PASS
ONLY ONE HUNDRED FIFTY SIX DAYS
TILL I'M DONE WITH FOURTH GRADE.

**MR. TWISSEL.** Hello, class. Hello? I wonder if we might do some spelling.

**CARLA & KID 2.** No!

**MR. TWISSEL.** How about some nice science?

**CARLA & KID 2.** No!

**MR. TWISSEL.** OK, kids. Let's draw pictures. Everybody take out a piece of paper.

*(A moment later, a fusillade of paper airplanes sails towards them –* **TWISSEL** *escapes. The bell rings.* **WILSON** *sings as behind him we go back to the school yard.)*

**KID 2.**

HEY THERE WILSON

**WILSON.**

PLEASE DON'T TALK TO ME

**CARLA.**

WANT TO PET THE TOAD?

**WILSON.** Nope! Too scary.

**KID 2.**

DO YOU WANT A COCA COLA?

**WILSON.**

I'M AFRAID IT MIGHT EXPLODE

**CARLA & KID 2.**

AHH, OO!

**WILSON.**

SOMETIMES I WISH I WASN'T SUCH A WIMP

**KIDS.**

AHH, OO!

**WILSON.**

BUT IT'S HARD TO BE BRAVE WHEN YOU'RE JUST A LITTLE
SHRIMP

I wish I could be tough and brave! Like a ninja! Or
a fireman! Or a ninja fireman – cool! But everything
is so scary around here. Especially my mean, terrible,
awful principal –

*(He turns around, and* **PRINCIPAL PURVIS** *has entered,
having changed out of his Mr. Twissel outfit during the
preceding.)*

Principal Purvis!

*(As* **WILSON** *sings the following, cruel* **PRINCIPAL
PURVIS** *stalks the schoolyard, tailed by his lackey,
prim* **MS. QUERN. PRINCIPAL PURVIS**, *beady-eyed and
uptight, always carries a coffee mug, which he sips from
as he barks orders, etc.)*

**WILSON.**

BUT PRINCIPAL PURVIS, HE'S THE WORST
OF THE PEOPLE WHO
SCARE ME, THAT GUY COMES FIRST
I'M PRETTY SURE HE HATES ME
HE MAKES ME SO AFRAID.

**PRINCIPAL PURVIS.**

I DON'T LIKE CHILDREN
GRUMBLE MUMBLE MUMBLE GRUMBLE GRUMBLE,
SIGH, COMPLAIN.

**WILSON.**

I WISH I COULD HIDE INSIDE A SHELL AND STAY TILL I
HEAR THE FINAL BELL
ONLY ONE HUNDRED FIFTY SIX DAYS TILL
I'M DONE WITH FOURTH…

*(The bell rings. **WILSON** shouts "yes!", shoulders his backpack, begins the walk home.)*

**WILSON.** *(cont.)*
> ONLY ONE HUNDRED FIFTY FIVE DAYS.
> ONLY ONE HUNDRED FIFTY FIVE DAYS
> ONLY ONE HUNDRED FIFTY FIVE DAYS
> TILL I'M DONE WITH FOURTH GRADE.

## Scene Two

## Wilson's House – Dining Room

*(WILSON sits at the dinner table with his MOM and DAD.)*

**DAD.** Wilson.

**MOM.** Wilson, honey.

**WILSON.** Yes?

**DAD.** Where are your glasses, dear?

**WILSON.** I, um – I lost them.

**MOM.** Again?!

**DAD.** Wilson! Money is very tight right now, young man.

**MOM.** And glasses don't grow on trees, dear.

**DAD.** No, indeed. Just leaves.

**MOM.** Yes. And flowers.

*(WILSON tunes them out, turns to the audience. MOM and DAD keep talking, not realizing he's not listening.)*

**WILSON.** I can't tell my parents that Carla broke my glasses. Again.

**DAD.** Plus fruit of course.

**MOM.** Right, fruit grows on trees. Fruit trees.

**WILSON.** And I can't tell them that when I told Principal Purvis, he punished me for fighting.

**MOM.** And tree bark.

**DAD.** Oh sure. Tree bark.

**WILSON.** Thank heaven this day is almost over. I just hope tomorrow doesn't bring anything too scary. If there's one thing I can't stand, it's surprises.

*(Suddenly, right behind WILSON, a pirate appears.)*

**UNCLE PIRATE.** *(by way of greeting)* Argh!

**WILSON.** *(very surprised)* Aah!

*(UNCLE PIRATE looks like the biggest trick or treater you've ever seen. He wears a pirate costume, with a big*

*black hat, a patch over one eye, a peg leg, a long red coat, a cutlass, and two old-fashioned flintlock pistols in his belt.* **WILSON** *is flabbergasted.)*

**DAD.** What in the – are you a pirate?

**UNCLE PIRATE.** Argh! Mighty perceptive of ya!

*(throwing his arm around* **MOM***)*

Emmy, m'dear, ya married a good un!

**DAD.** Darling? You know this person?

**MOM.** Yes. Dear, this is my long-lost brother.

**UNCLE PIRATE.** So I am indeed! Now shake hands and splice hearts, will ye?!

*(He gives* **DAD** *an enthusiastic handshake, during which* **WILSON** *turns to the audience with a gobsmacked expression.)*

**DAD.** Your brother? So he's – he's –

**WILSON.** My uncle!! Uncle Pirate!

*(***WILSON** *jumps in between* **DAD** *and* **UNCLE PIRATE** *and gives him a handshake of his own, turning into an embrace.)*

**UNCLE PIRATE.** Reckon that's true! I'm yer Uncle, and yer me very own nevvy.

**MOM.** But what are you doing here, Bob?

**UNCLE PIRATE.** I'm wonderin' if I kin bunk with you land-lubbers for a spell, just till I get me bearings?

**MOM.** Stay…with us?

**DAD.** Here?

**MOM.** Gee…

**WILSON.** Of course! Come on, Uncle Pirate! You can stay in my room.

*(He drags* **UNCLE PIRATE** *off.)*

**DAD.** I –

**MOM.** But –

## Scene Three

## Wilson's Room

(**WILSON** *bounces around the room excitedly.*)

**WILSON.** I can't believe it! A real pirate! In my own room! Sorry it smells like old socks.

**UNCLE PIRATE.** Don't apologize, nevvy! No better smell I kin think of, less'n it's old fish guts, rottin' in the noonday sun. Where do I put my bag?

**WILSON.** What's in it?

**UNCLE PIRATE.** Oh, you know. Treasure maps. Eye patches. Couple shark fins I be savin' for soup.

(*He slings it on the bed.*)

**WILSON.** I've never met a real pirate before. Do you have a nifty pirate name, like Blackbeard?

**UNCLE PIRATE.** (*as he puts down his things, makes himself comfortable*) I tried some out. I tried Black Bob. But the crew said it were only a copy of Blackbeard. Then I tried Polka Dot Bob, but the crew said that sounded funny. Finally I tried Desperate Evil Bob, but the crew said that were too long.

**WILSON.** So, how did you get here?

**UNCLE PIRATE.** That be a long story.

**WILSON.** OK.

**UNCLE PIRATE.** Which I'll tell ya now.

(*Underscore sneaks in.*)

I was the captain of my very own ship: *The Hyena of the Seas!* Only there were some *trouble.* With me crew.

**WILSON.** Trouble?

**UNCLE PIRATE.** Trouble!

(*sings:*)
MANY MOONS AGO I HAD ME A SHIP
THE HANDSOMEST EVER YOU SAW
WITH A BIG WIDE DECK AND FOUR BILLOWING SAILS
THAT FILLED EVERY LAST PERSON WITH AWE.

**UNCLE PIRATE.**

> I SANG YO HO HO AND A
> LA DA DEE DA!
> A PIRATE'S WHAT I'M MEANT TO BE
> I SANG YO HO HO AND A
> LA DA DEE DA!
> I'M LOVIN' ME LIFE ON THE SEA.

*(Enter* **3 CHORUS MEMBERS** *dressed as pirates.)*

**UNCLE PIRATE.**

| | |
|---|---|
| NOW MY CREW | **CREW.** |
| WAS GOOD, BUT THEY | WE WANT TREASURE! |
| SOMETIMES COMPLAINED | TREASURE, TREASURE, |
| THAT WE NEVER DID FIND | TREASURE, TREASURE, |
| ANY TREASURE! | BLECH |
| BUT I DIDN'T CARE MUCH | |
| ABOUT SILVER OR GOLD | |
| IT WAS SAILIN' THAT | |
| GAVE ME THE PLEASURE | |

**UNCLE PIRATE, WILSON, & CREW.**

> I SANG YO HO HO AND A
> LA DA DEE DA!
> A PIRATE'S WHAT I'M MEANT TO BE
> I SANG YO HO HO AND A
> LA DA DEE DA!
> I'M LOVIN' ME LIFE ON THE SEA.

**UNCLE PIRATE.**

| | |
|---|---|
| BUT ONE DAY ME OLD FOE | **WICKED LARRY.** |
|  WICKED LARRY | ARGH! |
| HE WANTED ME SHIP FOR | YES I DO! |
| HIS OWN | I'LL FIND US TREASURE |
| HE SAID: | IF YOU LET ME BE |
| AND THEY LEFT ME IN | CAPTAIN |
| ANTARCTICA, ALL ALONE | |
| THEY SANG: | |

**CREW.**
> YO HO HO AND A
> LA DA DEE DA!
> LET'S FIND US SOME GOLD TO UN-BURY
> THEY SANG YO HO HO AND A
> LA DA DEE DA!
> YOU STAY HERE. WE'LL GO WITH WICKED LARRY!

**UNCLE PIRATE.**
> I SANG YO HO HO AND A
> LA DA DEE DA
> I'VE LOSTED ME SHIP AND ME CREW.
> YO HO HO AND A
> LA DA DEE DA. NOW
> WHAT IS A PIRATE TO DO?

> *(Underscore continues, as…)*

**WILSON.** You were stranded in Antarctica! All by yourself?

**UNCLE PIRATE.** Not entirely.

> *(Suddenly enter **CAPTAIN JACK**, an adorable penguin with sneakers on.)*

**CAPTAIN JACK.** Hello, there.

**WILSON.** What the –

**UNCLE PIRATE.** Captain Jack, I'd like you to meet me nevvy, Wilson. We'll be bunkin' together a spell. Wilson, this is Captain Jack. He's a penguin.

**WILSON.** A talking penguin?

**CAPTAIN JACK.** That seems clear. Can I sleep in your refrigerator?

**WILSON.** Um, I guess so.

> *(He points towards the kitchen.)*

**CAPTAIN JACK.** Great. Night-night!

> *(**CAPTAIN JACK** waddles off.)*

> *(**WILSON** climbs into bed, as **UNCLE PIRATE** strings his hammock between the top bunk and the door.)*

**WILSON.** *(drifting off…)* It sure is fun being related to a pirate.

**UNCLE PIRATE.** And it sure is fun bein' one. Now it's time to be gettin' some shut-eye, lad.

**WILSON.** Good night, Uncle Pirate.

**UNCLE PIRATE.** Good night, nevvy.

    (**WILSON** *sleeps.* **UNCLE PIRATE** *sits with his old head crooked in his elbow, gazing out the window at the big yellow moon.*)

I SING YO HO HO AND A
LA DA DEE DA
I'VE LOSTED ME SHIP AND ME CREW.
YO HO HO AND A
LA DA DEE DA.
NOW WHAT IS A PIRATE TO DO?

## Scene Four

## In Wilson's Bedroom

*(The next morning.* **WILSON**'s *bedroom.* **UNCLE PIRATE** *is sleeping, snoring heavily in his hammock.)*

*(***WILSON*** is pacing. He looks worried.)*

**WILSON**. Uncle Pirate?

*(***UNCLE PIRATE*** snores.)*

I'm scared, Uncle Pirate.

*(***UNCLE PIRATE*** jolts awake.)*

**UNCLE PIRATE**. Scared! What is it? Sharks! Is it sharks?

**WILSON**. No, Uncle Pirate.

**UNCLE PIRATE**. *(disappointed)* Oh, well.

**WILSON**. See, I was sort of hoping you might stay here with us for a while, Uncle Pirate.

**UNCLE PIRATE**. Me, too, lad. Leastways until I can find a new crew and once again be a' prowlin' the high seas! Searchin' for treasure! Wrasslin' octopuses! With a yo ho ho and a –

**WILSON**. Uncle Pirate?

**UNCLE PIRATE**. Sorry.

**WILSON**. But I overheard Mom and Dad talking early this morning, before they went to work. First Dad said,

*(A spotlight opens up, elsewhere on stage, revealing* **WILSON**'s *parents.)*

**DAD**. You know, honey, this isn't a very big apartment.

**WILSON**. And then Mom said:

**MOM**. I know, dear.

**WILSON**. And then Dad said

**DAD**. We don't really have room for a pirate in here!

**WILSON**. And then Mom said:

**MOM**. I know, dear.

**WILSON.** And then Dad said:

**DAD.** Is that a penguin in the refrigerator?

**WILSON.** And then Mom said:

**MOM.** One problem at a time, dear.

**UNCLE PIRATE.** Sensible lassie, my sister.

*(The spotlight the parents are in disappears.)*

**WILSON.** Uncle Pirate, we don't have a lot of extra space, or a lot of extra money for a long-term house guest. I'm worried my folks won't let you stay, unless you can contribute to the household.

**UNCLE PIRATE.** Hurm. You mean like a job?

**WILSON.** Exactly. But what kind of job?

*(They pace.)*

**UNCLE PIRATE.** Hm.

**WILSON.** Hm.

*(**CAPTAIN JACK** enters and paces with them.)*

**CAPTAIN JACK.** Hm.

**WILSON.** You could work at the coffee shop, Stircrocks!

*(A barista's apron flies in, and on to **UNCLE PIRATE**.)*

You know: taking orders, making lattes, serving scones –

**UNCLE PIRATE.** Scones? Never! I made a sacred vow, many moons ago, upon the high seas of the Tahitian Coast, that on my life and honor, never would I serve *scones*.

**WILSON.** Seriously?

**UNCLE PIRATE.** Yup. What else ya got?

*(They pace.)*

**UNCLE PIRATE.** Hm.

**WILSON.** Hm.

**CAPTAIN JACK.** Hm.

**UNCLE PIRATE.** I can't just have any old job, ya see? I'm a pirate, nevvy, a pirate to me very bones! I need adventure! I need danger! I need scares!

**WILSON.** *(sarcastic)* You should come to my school. It's the scariest place in the world.

**UNCLE PIRATE.** School, eh?

**CAPTAIN JACK.** School!?!

*(He looks incredibly excited; he might even cast an excited glance at the audience. He runs off.* **WILSON** *and* **UNCLE PIRATE** *don't notice him running off.)*

**WILSON.** School scares me more than anything.

**UNCLE PIRATE.** Well that answers our question, then, laddy: I'll be comin' to yer school.

**WILSON.** Wait – Uncle Pirate, I don't know about that.

**UNCLE PIRATE.** I kin' find me a job at this scary ole school of yours…and while I'm at it, you know what I'll do? I'll *unscarify* it for ye.

**WILSON.** Unscarify?

**UNCLE PIRATE.** Unscarify! That's pirate slang! Meanin', "to make not scary anymore."

**WILSON.** You'd do that? For me?

**UNCLE PIRATE.** Of course! For the time bein' you're the only crew member I've got, and accordin' to Rule #2 of the International Pirate Code, I've got to do whatever I can to protect me crew mates.

**WILSON.** The International what-now?

**UNCLE PIRATE.** The International Pirate Code, lad!!

*(He pulls out an old paper.)*

Rule #1: Stand true to yourself! Rule #2: Stand true to your crew! Rule #3: When the sea gets rough, stand up 'n' be tough! Rule #4: Eye patches are fun, but optional.

**WILSON.** Really? That's in there?

*(***WILSON*** reaches for the paper.)*

**UNCLE PIRATE.** Rule #5: No touchin' the Code!

*(***CAPTAIN JACK*** returns, in sunglasses, a baseball cap, and a big backpack.)*

**CAPTAIN JACK.** Okay! I'm ready!

**WILSON.** You're coming to school too, Captain Jack?

**CAPTAIN JACK.** Oh, yes. School is the only place I can achieve my greatest dream in life.

**UNCLE PIRATE.** To win the Canary Island Tuna fish Eating Contest?

**CAPTAIN JACK.** No – my *other* greatest dream!

> *(bursts into song, as penguins are wont to do:)*

> I'VE GOT EVERY SWIMMING STROKE DOWN PAT
> I CAN BUILD A NEST IN NO TIME FLAT
> BUT ALL I WANNA BE ABLE TO DO
> IS READ, READ, READ, READ!

> I'VE GOT PERFECT PENGUIN-DIVE TECHNIQUE
> I CAN CATCH A FISH WITH JUST MY BEAK

**UNCLE PIRATE.** It's true.

**CAPTAIN JACK.**

> BUT ALL I WANNA BE ABLE TO DO
> IS READ!

> WHEN I CAN READ
> LEARNING NEW THINGS WON'T BE HARD
> I'LL BE THE FIRST
> PENGUIN WITH A LIBRARY CARD
> I'LL READ THE ENCYCLOPEDIA
> FROM AARDVARK TO ZEBRA AND THEN
> NO ONE WILL CALL ME BIRD BRAIN AGAIN!

> I CAN HOLD MY BREATH TEN MINUTES IF I TRY
> I CAN FLAP MY WINGS AND ALMOST FLY

**UNCLE PIRATE.** Almost!

**CAPTAIN JACK.**

> BUT ALL I WANNA BE ABLE TO DO IS READ!

> *(The number continues as the three heroes travel to Wilson's school, Very Elementary.)*

> IF I WAS EVER BITTER IT
> WAS BECAUSE I WAS ILLITERATE I
> COULDN'T DO THE ONE THING THAT I NEED
> GIMME BOOKS AND POEMS AND COMIC STRIPS CUZ
> THE WHOLE WORLD'S AT MY FLIPPER TIPS
> THE DAY I LEARN TO READ! I WANNA READ!

## Scene Five

## The Very Elementary School Schoolyard

*(The merry little band – pirate, penguin, and boy – now stand at the lip of the stage, looking out at the audience.)*

*(A basketball hoop appears behind them.)*

*(Sound cue: Loud, obnoxious children at play.)*

**WILSON.** Well, here's my school. Very Elementary.

**CAPTAIN JACK.** I'm so excited.

**WILSON.** Look out – there's mean Carla.

**CARLA.** I thought I broke those stupid glasses of yours.

**WILSON.** These are new ones. We buy them in bulk.

*(She leaves.)*

See? Everything is scary!

**UNCLE PIRATE.** I think you might be over-reactin', nevvy.

**WILSON.** Oh?

**UNCLE PIRATE.** Indeed. Most of the time, lad, being scared only serves ta make a person *more* scared. When half the time, there's nuthin' to be scared of in the first place. You understand?

**WILSON.** Yes.

**UNCLE PIRATE.** You sure?

**WILSON.** Yes.

**UNCLE PIRATE.** Luverly. Now –

*(**WILSON** lets out a shriek of fear, hides behind **UNCLE PIRATE**.)*

**WILSON.** Oh, no – here comes Principal Purvis!

**PRINCIPAL PURVIS.** Well, well, well.

**MS. QUERN.** Yes. Well, well, well.

**PRINCIPAL PURVIS.** What in God's name do you think you're doing, young man?

**WILSON.** I, uh– I –

**PRINCIPAL.** And who is this supposed to be?

**WILSON.** This is my uncle. Uncle Pirate.

**PRINCIPAL PURVIS.** Oh, is it. Ms. Quern, does the rulebook allow for pirates at school?

**MS. QUERN.** No, Principal Purvis, I do not believe that it does.

**CAPTAIN JACK.** Does it say anything about talking penguins?

**MS. QUERN.** That I will have to check.

(*She exits.*)

**PRINCIPAL PURVIS.** Young man? You have earned yourself detention.

**WILSON.** Detention?

**UNCLE PIRATE.** That won't be necessary, me hardy. The young man just brought me in for the ole – what do ye be callin' it? Show 'n' yell.

**WILSON.** Show and tell.

**UNCLE PIRATE.** Precisely.

**PRINCIPAL PURVIS.** Hmmm. Then I guess we'll let it go: *this time.* Next time you shan't be so lucky. And I'll be confiscating that sword, thank you very much.

(**PRINCIPAL PURVIS** *takes* **UNCLE PIRATE**'s *sword, and then exits.*)

**WILSON.** Phew! He's gone. Thanks, Uncle Pirate.

**UNCLE PIRATE.** Tis nuthin'. Now, what did you say that rapscallion's name was?

**WILSON.** Principal Purvis.

**UNCLE PIRATE.** I swear he looks a bit familiar to me. If I didn't know better –

(*The bell rings.*)

**WILSON.** Time to go to class.

**CAPTAIN JACK.** Oh boy oh boy oh boy!

## Scene Six

## The Fourth Grade Classroom

*(A light shift; the basketball hoops disappears and a chalkboard appears in its place.)*

*(Sound cue: A room full of the worst-behaved children in the world.)*

*(**UNCLE PIRATE**, **WILSON**, and **CAPTAIN JACK** are standing in the doorway, observing the terribly-behaved children. Maybe **UNCLE PIRATE** surveys them with a telescope.)*

**WILSON.** OK, so, the kid sitting on the other kid's head is Kevin. The kid getting his head sat on is Richard. And that's Betsy poking Mr. Goldfish, the class goldfish, with a stick.

**UNCLE PIRATE.** Blimey! An who be the captain of this ignoble vessel?

**WILSON.** You mean, the teacher? That's Mr. Twissel–here.

*(Suddenly they are joined by the frightened-looking teacher, **MR. TWISSEL**. He is clutching a short stack of note cards, which tremble in his hand.)*

**MR. TWISSEL.** Good morning. Hi. Sorry to bother you... could I, um...

*(A fusillade of paper airplanes sails towards them.)*

**CAPTAIN JACK.** This is terrible. How can I learn anything in a place like this?

**WILSON.** I told you not to get your hopes up.

**UNCLE PIRATE.** I've never seen such mollymockery in all my days!

**MR. TWISSEL.** Well, it's the best I can do! The parents are unhelpful, I have no administrative support, and the standardized tests? Forget about it. I'd like to see you do better, Mr. – Mr. – Pirate?

**WILSON.** Uncle Pirate, actually. Mr. Twissel, this is my uncle; he's a pirate captain.

**MR. TWISSEL.** Oh?

**WILSON.** And this is his friend, Captain Jack.

**CAPTAIN JACK.** I'm a talking penguin.

**MR. TWISSEL.** Is that right?

**WILSON.** Yes.

**MR. TWISSEL.** Well, then. Good news. You children have driven me completely around the bend. I am now going somewhere quiet to take a nice, long rest. I quit! And I'm NEVER coming back.

*(He flings his note cards up in the air and flees the room.)*

*(Sound cue: "All the kids cheered and jumped up and down.")*

**MR. TWISSEL.** Whee!

*(As* **WILSON,** **CAPTAIN JACK** *and* **UNCLE PIRATE** *watch, the room gets louder and louder. One by one, the other cast members streak across the stage in various attitudes of unholy mischief: On a pogo stick, doing cartwheels, juggling knives, whatever.)*

**WILSON.** Uh-oh. No teacher? Now we're in for it.

**UNCLE PIRATE.** Belaaaaaay!

*(Dead silence. The unruly classmates stop in their tracks.)*

**CARLA.** Did he say "belay?"

**KID 2.** What does "belay" mean?

**CARLA.** What smells like old calamari?

**UNCLE PIRATE.** I do! And thank you! And belay means "knock it off"! And I'll teach you another word, while we're at it: mollymockery. Which of you scurvy mop buckets knows *that* word?

*(silence)*

It means tomfoolery! High jinks! The drunken rioting of sailors on Greenland whalers. What I see before me at present is a crew lackin' a captain – and there's nothin' more despicable than that.

**WILSON.** Captain Jack! Are you thinking what I'm thinking?

**CAPTAIN JACK.** That Mr. Goldfish looks delicious? Yes!

**WILSON.** No!

*(turns to* **UNCLE PIRATE***)*

Uncle Pirate, why don't you be our new teacher! That can be your job.

**UNCLE PIRATE.** I? Teach?

**WILSON.** Of course. We need a captain, and you need a crew.

**UNCLE PIRATE.** But what if your teacher comes back?

**MR. TWISSEL.** *(from way off – recorded? – or delivered while the actor is backstage, changing into a kid)* Never! Never coming back!

**UNCLE PIRATE.** Very well young nevvy – I'll teach you and this lot of rogues to be pirates!

*(***KID 3*** *has run on at some point, or comes in now.)*

**KIDS.** Yay!

**WILSON.** Oh, that would be great! But I think you actually have to teach us *this* stuff.

*(***WILSON*** *hands* **UNCLE PIRATE** *the stack of note cards, lately abandoned by* **MR. TWISSEL.***)*

**KIDS.** Boo!

**UNCLE PIRATE.** Ah! Never fear. I reckon I can teach 'em both.

*(sings:)*

IT TAKES MIGHTY FINE LADS AND LASSES
TO SAIL ACROSS THE OCEAN
BUT HERE ALL I SEE
BE MOLLYMOCKERY, RUDENESS AND COMMOTION
AS SAILORS GO, YE'D BE THE WORST
SO THERE'S THINGS YE BEST BE LEARNIN' FIRST

**CARLA.** What?

**KID 3.** Yeah – what?

**UNCLE PIRATE.**

> WHAT IF WE BE OUT AT SEA
> AND WE DISCOVER TREASURE?
> WE'D HAVE TO DIVIDE IT UP
> IN SOMEWHAT EQUAL MEASURE.
> IF SOMEONE GETS LESS THAN SOMEONE ELSE
> YOU'D HAVE TO FACE HER WRATH.
> IF YOU WANT TO BE A PIRATE THEN
> YOU'VE GOT TO KNOW YOUR MATH!
> YOU'VE GOT TO KNOW YOUR MATH!
> YOU'VE GOT TO KNOW YOUR MATH!
> IF YOU WANT TO BE A PIRATE THEN
> YOU'VE GOT TO KNOW YOUR MATH!

**UNCLE PIRATE.** Good! You! Purple shirt! Three times six!

**KID 2.** Uh – 18!

**UNCLE PIRATE.** Two eyes minus one?

**KID 3.** Uh – one?

**UNCLE PIRATE.** Right!

> *(He slaps an eye patch on the kid and turns back to the lesson plan.)*

**UNCLE PIRATE.** Ok! Social studies!

**KIDS.** What?! No!

**UNCLE PIRATE.** Quiet! Listen!

> *(sings:)*

> WHAT IF WE BE OUT AT SEA
> AND NEEDED SOME DIRECTIONS?
> EVERYONE'S GOT STOMACH ACHES
> AND NASTY EAR INFECTIONS.
> AND IF WE DON'T GET TO SHORE REAL QUICK
> OUR MAST IS GONNA SNAP
> IF YOU WANT TO BE A PIRATE THEN
> YOU'VE GOT TO READ A MAP.
>
> YOU'VE GOT TO READ A MAP!
> YOU'VE GOT TO READ A MAP!
> IF YOU WANT TO BE A PIRATE
> YOU'VE GOT TO READ A MAP!

**CARLA.**
> THERE'S SO MUCH TO KNOW
> IF I WANT TO BE A SAILOR

**KID 2.**
> WHAT FISH CAN I EAT?

**CARLA.**
> WHAT STAR POINTS NORTH?

**KID 3.**
> AND WHAT'S A GREENLAND WHALER?
>
> (**UNCLE PIRATE** *produces a parchment document from his pocket.*)

**UNCLE PIRATE.** Now it's time to be tellin' ye the most important thing of all – if you're gonna be a pirate, you've got to obey the International Pirate Code! Repeat after me: Rule #1: Stand true to yourself!

**KIDS.** Stand true to yourself!

**UNCLE PIRATE.** Rule #2! Stand true to your crew!

**KIDS.** Stand true to your crew!

**UNCLE PIRATE.** Rule #3! When the sea gets rough, stand up 'n' be tough!

**KIDS.** When the sea gets rough, stand up and be tough!

**UNCLE PIRATE.** Rule #4. Eye patches are fun, but optional.

**KIDS.** Eye patches are…really? That's in there?

**UNCLE PIRATE.** Now dance, mateys! Dance!

**KIDS.** Dance?

**UNCLE PIRATE.** I'll show ya!

> (*Everyone does the international pirate dance.*)

**UNCLE PIRATE, WILSON, & KIDS.**
> WHAT IF WE BE OUT AT SEA
> AND NORTH WINDS START A BLOWIN'?
> WE'D BE GLAD FOR ALL OF THE
> EARTH SCIENCE WE BE KNOWIN'.
> THERE'S SO MUCH YOU NEED TO LEARN SO JUST
> REMEMBER THIS ONE RULE
> IF YOU WANT TO BE A PIRATE

**UNCLE PIRATE, WILSON, & KIDS.** *(cont.)*
> YOU'VE GOT TO GO TO SCHOOL!
> YOU'VE GOT TO GO TO SCHOOL!
> YOU'VE GOT TO GO TO SCHOOL!
> IF YOU WANT TO BE A PIRATE THEN
> YOU'VE GOT TO GO TO SCHOOL!
> YOU'VE GOT TO LEARN TO BE A PIRATE!

*(Song ends jubilantly.)*

*(***UNCLE PIRATE*** then rolls up the parchment carefully.)*

**UNCLE PIRATE.** Here, nevvy, you hold this for me, will ye?

**WILSON.** I thought no one was allowed to touch the Code but the captain.

**UNCLE PIRATE.** *(proudly handing the doc to* **WILSON***)* Not lessin' he be the First Mate.

**WILSON.** Wow! Me? really? A First Mate!

**UNCLE PIRATE.** There's nuthin' to it, laddy. A First Mate is TOUGH and SMART and can navigate through any sitch-ee-ation. You think you kin' do all that?

**WILSON.** I don't know, Uncle Pirate.

*(As they speak, mean* **CARLA** *is entering.)*

**UNCLE PIRATE.** Well, let's find out…hey, you! Carla! Wilson here says yer the no-account grog-guzzlin' son of a squid!

*(***UNCLE PIRATE*** ducks behind a chalkboard.)*

## Scene Seven

*(Continuing.* **CARLA** *angrily stomps up to* **WILSON**.*)*

**CARLA.** What did you call me?

**WILSON.** To tell you the truth, I have absolutely no idea.

**CARLA.** Doesn't matter. I'm gonna break your glasses anyway.

**WILSON.** But you can't! I brought a pirate to school. I'm the First Mate. I'm…I'm…

*(daringly)*

I'm cool now.

**CARLA.** What, you think just because your uncle is a pirate, I'm going to stop breaking your glasses? That's not very logimical.

**WILSON.** You mean, logical.

**CARLA.** It's just that sort of condescending comment that makes me excited to punch you in the face. Let me just roll up my sleeves.

**WILSON.** *(to himself)* Why aren't I running away?

**CARLA.** Let me just get these sleeves nice and rolled up…

**WILSON.** I should really take advantage of this long pause to escape.

**CARLA.** …new shirt…extra-long sleeves…hmm…

**WILSON.** And yet –

**CARLA.** …there we go, nice and rolled…

**WILSON.** …oh my gosh!

*(to* **CARLA***)*

I'm not afraid!

**CARLA.** What?! Why not!

**WILSON.** Because – what was it again?

*(thinks for a moment, and then repeats what* **UNCLE PIRATE** *said earlier:)*

**WILSON.** Most of the time, being scared only makes some-one more scared. Half the time, there's nothing to be scared of in the first place.

**CARLA.** What?!? But you have to be afraid of me.

**WILSON.** Don't you see? You're only a bully because you're afraid of being nice.

**CARLA.** No, goofus. I'm a bully because I'm really good at it.

*(sings:)*

LOTS OF THINGS ARE HARD FOR ME
LIKE SPELLING AND GEOGRAPHY.
I SEE BLANKS ON TESTS AND I CAN'T FILL THEM.
I ALSO DON'T HAVE MANY FRIENDS
BUT EVERYONE AT LEAST PRETENDS
TO LIKE ME WHEN THEY THINK I'M GONNA KILL THEM.

PUNCH! KICK! WHAM!
I START SWINGING WITH A
POW! BOOM! BAM!
TIL YOUR EARS ARE RINGING
AND YOU'RE ALL BEGGING ME TO QUIT.
THUMP! SPANK! SLAM!
I FEEL IMPORTANT WHEN I HIT.

**WILSON.** Oh, Carla. All you need is a way to put your nega-tive energies toward a positive task!

**CARLA.** Huh?

**WILSON.**

IT'S MUST BE PRETTY LONELY TO
HAVE EVERYONE BE SCARED OF YOU
WOULDN'T IT BE NICER TO BE FRIENDLY?

**CARLA.**

NO, REALLY I'D PREFER TO SEE
THEM SQUIRM AROUND IN AGONY
THAN HAVE THE WHOLE FOURTH GRADE GO FACEBOOK
FRIEND ME.

**CARLA.** *(cont.)*

> WHAP! SLAP! WHACK!
> COME LET ME SHOW YOU
> HI YA! SMACK!
> HOW I TAE KWON DO YOU
> I THINK THAT YOU'D HAVE TO ADMIT
> WHOOSH, SLASH, CRACK!
> I GET RESPECTED WHEN I HIT.

**WILSON.**

> WE ALL WANT TO FIT IN, CARLA.
> NO ONE LIKES TO BE REJECTED.
> BUT THERE ARE OTHER WAYS TO FEEL IMPORTANT
> You just need someone to help, instead of someone to hurt!

**CARLA.** Yeah, but who am I going to be able to help?

*(Just then, **CAPTAIN JACK** happens by, singing:)*

**CAPTAIN JACK.**

> ALL I WANNA BE ABLE TO DO IS READ!

**WILSON.** Perfect!

**CAPTAIN JACK.** Oh, hello. I didn't see you there.

**CARLA.** No! No, way!

**WILSON.** Of course, Carla! *You* can teach Captain Jack to read!

**CARLA.** I'm not good at reading. I'm a year behind.

**CAPTAIN JACK.** Do you know the alphabet?

**CARLA.** Is that the thing where all the letters used to make words are recited in sequence?

**WILSON.** Yes.

**CARLA.** Then, yeah.

**CAPTAIN JACK.** Oh! Show me how it works! Please!

**WILSON.** Carla, what about the International Pirate Code?

**CARLA.** I don't want to wear an eye patch.

**WILSON.** You have to face your fears! When the sea gets rough, stand up 'n' be tough!

(**CARLA** *summons her nerve…turns to the penguin… and…*)

**CARLA.** *(sings:)*
A! B! C!

**WILSON.**
YOU CAN DO IT, CARLA!

**CARLA.**
E! F! G!

**WILSON.**
YOU SKIPPED ONE BUT THAT'S OK

**CARLA.**
H! I! J! K! FOLLOW MY LEAD
L M N O P

**CAPTAIN JACK.**
THIS IS EXACTLY WHAT I NEED

**WILSON & JACK.**
IT'S NOT AS HARD AS IT LOOKS
INSTEAD OF HITTING PEOPLE, HIT THE BOOKS

**CARLA.**
I CAN DO THIS! I CAN DO THIS!

**WILSON & JACK.**
GO AND TEACH HIM (ME) HOW TO READ!

**CARLA.** All right, penguin. You've got yourself a deal.

*(Song buttons.)*

*(The school bell rings.* **UNCLE PIRATE** *pokes his head in.)*

## Scene Eight

## The Fourth Grade Classroom

*(Meanwhile!* **MS. QUERN** *and* **PRINCIPAL PURVIS** *prowl the school grounds.)*

**PRINCIPAL PURVIS.** Ms. Quern!

**MS. QUERN.** Yes, Principal Purvis?

**PRINCIPAL PURVIS.** Have you noticed there is something a bit unusual about Mr. Twissel's room.

**MS. QUERN.** I have indeed, Principal Purvis. The clock is 45 seconds fast, and the pencil sharpener looks like it hasn't been emptied in days.

**PRINCIPAL PURVIS.** I meant the singing! The loud, happy sea shanties coming out of that classroom!

**MS. QUERN.** Ah. Right. I noticed that also.

**PRINCIPAL PURVIS.** In fact, Ms. Quern, if I didn't know better, I'd think a pirate was teaching that class.

**MS. QUERN.** A pirate! Heavens to Betsy!

**PRINCIPAL PURVIS.** Do you think it's possible?

**MS. QUERN.** Well, there's only one way to find out.

**PRINCIPAL PURVIS.** Yes! I'll go down to Mr. Twissel's room and see for myself!

**MS. QUERN.** Oh. Yes. I guess that would also work.

*(He gives her a suitably exasperated expression, and departs!)*

## Scene Nine

## The Fourth Grade Classroom

**UNCLE PIRATE.**
> WHAT IF WE BE OUT AT SEA WITH ENEMIES TO WRESTLE?
> CARLA NEEDS ENOUGH STEEL WIRE TO PROTECT OUR
>     VESSEL
> SUDDENLY A HUGE GANG OF HUNGRY SHARKS BEGIN TO
>     SWIM AT HER
> IF YOU WANT TO BE A PIRATE, YOU'VE GOT TO FIND
>     PERIMETER
> YOU'VE GOT TO FIND THE PERIMETER

**KIDS & UNCLE PIRATE.**
> YOU'VE GOT TO FIND THE PERIMETER
> IF YOU WANT TO BE A PIRATE THEN YOU'VE GOT TO FIND
>     THE...

> (**PRINCIPAL PURVIS** *bursts in, interrupting the song...*)

**KIDS.** What they – I was just getting it – [etc.]

**PRINCIPAL PURVIS.** I knew it!

**UNCLE PIRATE.** You again, is it? Gar, but you look familiar, matey – you sure I don't know ye from somewheres?

**PRINCIPAL.** No! I don't know anyone. Wilson, I thought I told you pirates were not permitted in my school.

**WILSON.** I – well – gee, I –

**UNCLE PIRATE.** Don't be tremulous, Wilson. Haven't I taught ya nothin'? What can we do for you, Principal Puffin??

**PRINCIPAL PURVIS.** You can march those ugly boots of yours out of this classroom, the sooner the better. And it's PURVIS. Principal Lawrence P. Purvis, and no overgrown leprechaun with a Jolly Roger hat and a smelly beard is going to teach in my school.

**WILSON.** But – but –

> (**WILSON** *steps forward,* bravely.)

**WILSON.** With all due respect, Principal Purvis…we like having Uncle Pirate as our teacher! Don't we, guys?

**CARLA.** Yeah!

**CAPTAIN JACK.** Yeah!

**PRINCIPAL PURVIS.** You like it?

**WILSON.** Yes. We're learning – and we're happy.

**PRINCIPAL PURVIS.** You're *happy*? The one thing I will not tolerate in my school is happy children!

*(As he sings, he goes about the classroom, and makes them spit out their gum, comb their hair, stand up straight, etc.)*

*(***KID 2*** has to leave during this somewhere, to come back as* **QUERN**, *below.)*

*(sings:)*

I DON'T LIKE CHILDREN.
IT SCARES ME WHEN THEY WIGGLE
AND THEY GIGGLE AND HAVE FUN.
I DON'T LIKE CHILDREN.
THEY REALLY DO DISTURB ME
AND PRETURB ME, EVERY ONE.
THEY LEAVE THEIR GREASY HANDPRINTS
ON EVERYTHING THEY TOUCH. Ew.
I DISLIKE THEM SO MUCH.

SO THAT'S WHY I BECAME A PRINCIPAL!
A NASTY, WICKED PRINCIPAL!
THE GREATEST THING A KID-LOATHING GUY COULD BE.
AND BECAUSE I AM NOW A PRINCIPAL
I CAN MAKE THE CHILDREN FEEL
AS TIRED, ANGRY, OLD, AND ANNOYED AS ME!

I DON'T LIKE CHILDREN.
THEY REALLY DO ANNOY ME AND I
WISH THEY'D GO AWAY
I DON'T LIKE CHILDREN
SO I CASH IN ON THE PASSION
I DISLIKE THEM WITH EACH DAY

**PRINCIPAL PURVIS.** *(cont.)*

   I'M PAID TO MAKE THEM QUIET
   IT FILLS MY HEART WITH GLEE. Hee Hee!
   I DON'T LIKE CHILDREN. Sit up straight!
   DON'T LIKE... Don't sit so straight!

   DON'T LIKE 'EM DON'T LIKE 'EM
   DON'T LIKE 'EM DON'T LIKE 'EM
   DON'T LIKE 'EM DON'T LIKE 'EM
   DON'T LIKE 'EM DON'T LIKE 'EM

   I DON'T LIKE
   CHILDREN!

   (**UNCLE PIRATE** *bellies up to* **PRINCIPAL PURVIS.**)

**UNCLE PIRATE.** Well, I'm sorry you don't like the way I be teachafyin' these young ragamuffins, Principal Purplepants.

**PRINCIPAL PURVIS.** Purvis.

**UNCLE PIRATE.** But I'm afeared there ain't much you kin do ta stop me.

**PRINCIPAL PURVIS.** We'll see about that, won't we? We'll just see about that.

   (*He storms out, leaving his coffee mug behind.*)

**WILSON.** Oh, dear. Uncle Pirate, if Principal Purvis makes you leave, *then* what are we going to do?

   (**MS. QUERN**, *meek and timid, enters the room.*)

**UNCLE PIRATE.** Thar you go again, Wilson, being scared when there's no call to be.

**MS. QUERN.** Pardon me. I was just looking for Principal Purvis. I have his tunafish sandwich.

**CAPTAIN JACK.** Tunafish?

**WILSON.** But Uncle Pirate, don't you –

**MS. QUERN.** Whoa…hey…

   (**CAPTAIN JACK** *has sidled up to* **MS. QUERN** *and made a rude grab for the tunafish sandwich. In doing so, he knocks her glasses to the ground.*)

   My glasses!

**WILSON**. Oh, dear Uncle Pirate, what are we – Uncle Pirate?

> *(But **UNCLE PIRATE** is a bit distracted – because **MS. QUERN** looks up from the ground, glasses-less.)*

**MS. QUERN**. Oh, and my hair is a mess! Darn penguin!

> *(She lets down her hair and tosses it out. **UNCLE PIRATE**'s old pirate eyes drink her in as she looks about the room.)*

> *(A trill, a lingering exchanged look, the very heavens seem to sigh. **UNCLE PIRATE** takes the sandwich away from **CAPTAIN JACK** and returns it to her.)*

**MS. QUERN**.

> MY MOTHER SAID NEVER FALL FOR A PIRATE.
> SHE SAID "MS QUERN, DON'T YOU DARE
> EVER FALL FOR A PIRATE."
> THEY'RE STINKY AND SCARY
> AND TOOTHLESS AND HAIRY
> AND SO...
> I SAID I WOULD NOT FALL FOR A PIRATE,
> NO MATTER WHAT HE DOES.

**UNCLE PIRATE**. Bob. Desperate Evil Wicked Bob. At yer service, m'lady.

**MS. QUERN**.

> BUT THEN THERE HE WAS.
> LIKE A NICE WARM COFFEE CUP.
> LIKE A STAPLER THAT NEVER JAMS UP,
> FROM THE START
> HE CAME ARGH-ING
> AND SWASHBUCKLING INTO MY HEART.

> Hello. My name is Quern. Ms. Quern.

**UNCLE PIRATE**. A pleasure. I'm the new fourth grade instructifier.

**MS. QUERN**. A pleasure. And instructifier isn't a word.

**UNCLE PIRATE**. Aren't you a clever lassy. Clever and...beautiful.

**UNCLE PIRATE.**
> SECRETARY!
> SECRETARY!
> SO PURDY AND LOVELY IS SHE.
> SECRETARY!
> MY HEART ONCE BELONGED TO THE SEA
> BUT THEN THERE SHE BE!
> LIKE A SAIL WITHOUT ANY CUTS
> LIKE A JEWEL IN A PILE OF GUTS
> FROM THE START
> SHE COLATED AND FAXED HER WAY
> INTO MY HEART.

*(They sing in counterpoint.)*

| **MS. QUERN.** | **UNCLE PIRATE.** |
|---|---|
| MY MOTHER SAID NEVER<br>    FALL FOR A PIRATE. | SECRETARY! |
| SHE SAID "MS QUERN,<br>    DON'T YOU DARE | SECRETARY! |
| EVER FALL FOR A PIRATE." | SO PURDY AND LOVELY IS<br>    SHE! |
| THEY'RE STINKY AND SCARY | SECRETARY! |
| AND TOOTHLESS AND<br>    HAIRY | MY SOUL ONCE BELONGED<br>    TO THE SEA |
| AND SO… | |
| I SAID I WOULD NOT FALL<br>    FOR A PIRATE, | |
| NO MATTER WHAT HE<br>    DOES. | |

**BOTH.**
> BUT THEN THERE HE WAS (SHE BE)!

**MS. QUERN.**
> LIKE A NICE WARM COFFEE CUP

**UNCLE PIRATE.**
> LIKE A SAIL WITH NO CUTS

**MS. QUERN.**
> LIKE A STAPLER THAT NEVER JAMS UP UP

**UNCLE PIRATE.**

LIKE A JEWEL IN GUTS

**BOTH.**

AND I WONDER, COULD HE/SHE
LOVE ME TOO? OH
WHAT IS A PIRATE/SECRETARY TO DO?

**MS. QUERN.**

PIRATE…

**UNCLE PIRATE.**

SECRETARY!

*(Both of them sigh.* **WILSON** *is trying to get* **UNCLE PIRATE***'s attention, when…)*

### Scene Ten

*(Continuing.* **PRINCIPAL PURVIS** *bursts back in. Bursts!)*

**PRINCIPAL PURVIS.** A-ha!

**UNCLE PIRATE.** Shiver me timbers!

**PRINCIPAL PURVIS.** Well, Uncle Pirate – if you won't listen to reason, perhaps you'll listen to…*THIS!*

*(He produces a long sword.)*

**UNCLE PIRATE.** Well, I'll be the son of a squid. You dare to challenge me, a real-live pirate captain, to a sword fight?

**PRINCIPAL PURVIS.** Yes!

**UNCLE PIRATE.** In front of me own crew!

**PRINCIPAL PURVIS.** Yes!

**UNCLE PIRATE.** When I don't even have a sword?

*(***CAPTAIN JACK*** *leaps forward with one of those long chalkboard pointers.)*

**CAPTAIN JACK.** Here you go, Uncle Pirate.

**UNCLE PIRATE.** Perfect. *En guard,* Principal Purplepants!

*(They fight.)*

**CARLA.** THIS IS AWESOME.

**WILSON.** Wow – Principal Purvis is a surprisingly good sword fighter. How odd…

*(…dramatically,* **PURVIS** *gets the upper hand, knocks the pointer from* **UNCLE PIRATE***'s hand.)*

**CARLA.** Yeah! Get 'im!

**MS. QUERN.** Eek! Careful!

**PRINCIPAL PURVIS.** I've got you now!

**UNCLE PIRATE.** Not as long as I've got this…this…

**CAPTAIN JACK.** Here ya go!

**UNCLE PIRATE.** Dry erase marker!

*(They fight!)*

**CARLA.** Yeah! Get 'im! That's the stuff! [etc]

**MS. QUERN.** Oo! Be careful! The eyes are the most vulnerable part of the body! [etc]

(**PRINCIPAL PURVIS** *again gets the upper hand, knocks the dry erase marker from* **UNCLE PIRATE***'s hand.*)

**PRINCIPAL PURVIS.** *Now* I've got you!

**UNCLE PIRATE.** Not as long as I've got this…this…

**CAPTAIN JACK.** *(hands him a thick book)* Here you go!

**UNCLE PIRATE.** This…*Topographical Atlas of the Former Soviet Union!*

(*They fight, sword versus geography textbook. For a moment,* **UNCLE PIRATE** *takes the upper hand.*)

I've got you now, Lawrence P. Purvis!

(*The fighting continues.*)

(*Suddenly,* **PRINCIPAL PURVIS** *reverses* **UNCLE PIRATE***'s grip, and now has the upper hand; perhaps his boot is on* **UNCLE PIRATE***'s neck, his sword raised dramatically in the air.*)

**WILSON.** Wicked Larry!

**UNCLE PIRATE.** *(strained, from under the boot)* I knew I knew ye from somewhere.

(**WICKED LARRY** *steps off* **UNCLE PIRATE***'s neck, backs away still wielding the sword.*)

**PURVIS/LARRY.** Blimey! How did ye' crack me secret, you scalawag?

**WILSON.** Well, first of all, where would an elementary school principal get so good at sword fighting? And Uncle Pirate kept saying you looked familiar. AND there's the simple fact of your name – Lawrence. As in, Larry.

**CAPTAIN JACK.** Also, this coffee mug says "Wicked Larry, Pirate of the Month, October 2004."

**CARLA.** Good reading, Captain Jack!

**PURVIS/LARRY.** Argh! I don't know why I kept that thing. It be true! The crew mutinied against me, too, and I ended up right here at this self-same elementarary school!

**CAPTAIN JACK.** That's quite a coincidence.

**PURVIS/LARRY.** Cram it, penguin.

(*looks at* **UNCLE PIRATE**)

Now you listen ta me! Bein' a principal is the cushiest job I ever did have, and you ain't gonna take it from me! I am the *captain* of this elementary school, and as the captain I am in charge of everyone 'round here: includin' you.

(*He steps belly to belly with* **UNCLE PIRATE**.)

By the power vested in me by the International Pirate Code, I *order* you to leave.

**UNCLE PIRATE.** Argh!

(**WILSON** *stands up bravely at his uncle's side.*)

**WILSON.** Nice try! No way is Uncle Pirate going to just... Uncle Pirate?

**UNCLE PIRATE.** The Code is the Code, Wilson: If he's orderin' me to be off, then off I must be.

**CARLA.** What?

**CAPTAIN JACK.** You can't!

**WILSON.** We need you.

(*quietly:*)

*I* need you.

**UNCLE PIRATE.** I'm sorry.

(**UNCLE PIRATE** *stops at the door. A moment – what will he do? He hangs his head, takes off his pirate hat, and turns to go.*)

**MS. QUERN.** Uncle Pirate! No...

## Scene Eleven

## Stircrock's Coffee Shop

(**UNCLE PIRATE**, *in the barista's apron, addresses the audience directly.*)

**UNCLE PIRATE.** Welcome to Stircrock's. What can I be gettin' for you?

**CUSTOMER.** Let's see. How are the scones?

**UNCLE PIRATE.** Scones?!!

*(blackout)*

## Scene Twelve

### The Fourth Grade Classroom

*(The next day.)*

*(Sound cue: A room full of the worst-behaved children in the world.)*

*(**WILSON**, **CARLA**, and **CAPTAIN JACK** are in the front row.)*

**MS. QUERN.** Hello? Hello everyone. Principal Wicked Larry has asked me to teach this class until such time as a suitable fourth grade teacher can be located – or until Mr. Twissel should return.

**MR. TWISSEL.** *(from way off)* Never! Never coming back!

**WILSON.** This is ridiculous.

*(He leaps out of his chair.)*

We have to do something!

**MS. QUERN.** Now, Wilson. We all wish Uncle Wonderful – Pirate – would come back. But we need to face facts.

**WILSON.** Do we, Ms. Quern? Do we?

*(sings:)*

UNCLE PIRATE'S DOWN AND OUT
AND SEEMS TO BE DEJECTED.

**CAPTAIN JACK.**

IT LOOKS FOR ONCE LIKE HE'S THE ONE
WHO NEEDS TO BE PROTECTED.

**WILSON.**

IT'S STRANGE WHEN YOU HAVE TO HELP THE GUY
WHO USUALLY HELPS YOU.

**CAPTAIN JACK.**

WHAT'RE WE GONNA DO?

**WILSON.**

WE'RE GONNA
FOLLOW THE PIRATE CODE.
WE FOLLOW THE PIRATE CODE.
CUZ WHEN YOUR MATE'S IN TROUBLE
THEN ON THE DOUBLE
WE GET IN PIRATE MODE

*(**CAPTAIN JACK** leaps to his feet, and he and **WILSON** shake hands [flippers].)*

**WILSON & CAPTAIN JACK.**

>AND HELP OUR CREWMATES WHEN THEY'RE IN NEED
>WE NEVER WOULD LAUGH OR SCOFF
>I'LL LEND YOU A HAND IF SOMEONE BIT YOURS OFF
>BECAUSE WE FOLLOW THE PIRATE CODE!

>*(**WILSON** rallies the troops:)*

**WILSON.** Rule #1!

**CAPTAIN JACK.** Stand true to yourself!

**CAPTAIN JACK & WILSON.** Rule #2!

**ALL.** Stand true to your crew!

**CAPTAIN JACK.**

>FRIENDS DON'T LET THEIR FRIENDS GET CHOMPED BY SHARKS

**CARLA.**

>OR STAND BY WHEN THEY HEAR RUDE REMARKS

**MS. QUERN.**

>FRIENDS WON'T EVER LET YOU FEEL IGNORED

**ALL.**

>OR LET EACH OTHER GO OVERBOARD, BECAUSE THEY
>FOLLOW THE PIRATE CODE.
>WE FOLLOW THE PIRATE CODE.
>CUZ WHEN THE GUY WHO LEADS YOU
>DECIDES HE NEEDS YOU

>YOU GET IN PIRATE MODE
>YOU HAVE TO FOLLOW THE PIRATE CODE
>I'M SURE THAT YOU WOULD AGREE
>IF YOU'VE GOT A PEG LEG YOU CAN LEAN ON ME
>BECAUSE WE FOLLOW THE PIRATE CODE!
>*(As they sing, they travel, and burst into the coffee shop where **UNCLE PIRATE** is working.)*

**UNCLE PIRATE.** Welcome to Stircrocks, can I – shiver me timbers!!

**ALL.**

>FOLLOW, FOLLOW, FOLLOW
>FOLLOW THE CODE!
>FOLLOW THE CODE!
>FOLLOW THE PIRATE CODE!

## Scene Thirteen

*(continuing)*

**WILSON.** Uncle Pirate! We're here to bring you back.

**CARLA.** School isn't the same without you.

**MS. QUERN.** The whole world is dark, absent the bright light of your smile.

**KID 3.** Lemme get a triple skim machiato, no-whip.

**UNCLE PIRATE.** Argh! Wicked Larry's the captain, and I must do as he says. I must obey the International Pirate Code.

**WILSON.** Only if you're a pirate.

**UNCLE PIRATE.** What?

**WILSON.** Quit your old life! Come back to school! Be our teacher, from now on!

**UNCLE PIRATE.** But Wilson, to give up the life of the sea, the only life I ever known. I...I'm...

**WILSON.** You're scared. And that's OK. I used to be scared all the time. Until you came along...

*(sings:)*

TODAY MIGHT TURN OUT AWESOME
OR MAYBE NOT SO GREAT.
STUFF MIGHT GET TOUGH, BUT
I AM NOT AFRAID.

YESTERDAY IS OVER,
TOMORROW HAS TO WAIT
I'M HERE RIGHT NOW, AND
I'M NOT AFRAID.

SITTING IN YOUR ROOM
HOPING THINGS GET BETTER
NEVER MAKES YOUR PROBLEMS GO AWAY.
SOME THINGS TURN OUT EASY
SOME ARE REALLY HARD.
I'LL DO MY BEST AND IT'LL BE OK.

**WILSON.** *(cont.)*

> WE DON'T KNOW WHAT'LL HAPPEN.
> WE DON'T KNOW WHAT COMES NEXT.
> IT MIGHT BE GATORS, MIGHT BE GATORADE.
> BUT THERE'S NOTHING TO BE SCARED OF,
> AND I AM NOT AFRAID.

**ALL.**

> NO, THERE'S NOTHING TO BE SCARED OF,
> AND I AM NOT AFRAID.

**CAPTAIN JACK.** Why, I used to be afraid of pirates…till I met the most wonderful pirate of all.

**CARLA.** And *I* used to be afraid of being nice to people.

**KID 3.** And I used to be afraid of *her.*

**MS. QUERN.** And was afraid of never meeting someone special. With that certain calamari smell.

**ALL.** *(and, eventually, **UNCLE PIRATE**)*

> SITTING IN YOUR ROOM
> HOPING THINGS GET BETTER
> NEVER MAKES YOUR PROBLEMS GO AWAY.
> SOME THINGS TURN OUT EASY
> SOME ARE REALLY HARD.
> BUT I'LL DO MY BEST, AND IT'LL BE OK.
> WE DON'T KNOW WHAT'LL HAPPEN.
>
> WE DON'T KNOW WHAT COMES NEXT.
> IT MIGHT BE GATORS, MIGHT BE GATORADE.
> BUT THERE'S NOTHING TO BE SCARED OF,
> AND I AM NOT AFRAID.
> NO, THERE'S NOTHING TO BE SCARED OF,
> AND I AM NOT AFRAID.

*(As the song ends, they have arrived back at school, and **UNCLE PIRATE** has removed his pirate hat and picked up his chalk.)*

## Scene Fourteen

*(continuing)*

**WILSON.** Oh, hi. I'm Wilson. And I'm not hiding – I don't hide from anything. Not anymore! Hey, guys.

**CARLA.** …the…

**CAPTAIN JACK.** …the…

**CARLA.** …end! Great work!

**CAPTAIN JACK.** Thanks.

**CARLA.** And that's *War and Peace.*

> *(**UNCLE PIRATE** enters, with chalk, standing before dry erase board.)*

**UNCLE PIRATE.** Arrgh! Mornin' children! Who be ready for some learnifyin'!

**KIDS.** Yay!

**UNCLE PIRATE.** Today we'll be learnin' anatomy!

**KIDS.** Boo!

**UNCLE PIRATE.** Of sharks!

**KIDS.** Yay!

**WILSON.** Yup, Uncle Pirate is the permanent fourth grade teacher, and are darn good one, too. Oh, and guess what else?

> *(**MS. QUERN** enters, on her cell phone. **UNCLE PIRATE** looks at her beatifically.)*

**MS. QUERN.** Good morning, Uncle Fiancé.

**UNCLE PIRATE.** Good morning, Secretary of my Heart.

**WILSON.** Except Ms. Quern *isn't* a secretary – not anymore.

**MS. QUERN.** Larry! Wicked Larry! Wicked Secretary Larry!

**WICKED LARRY.** Yes, Principal Quern?

**MS. QUERN.** Take a memo! Dear parents, for our field trip on Thursday, life vests *will* be provided, but…

> *(**WICKED LARRY** looks at the audience, sighs with defeated exasperation.)*

**WILSON.** Good morning, Captain Jack! I mean…

*(with a wink to the audience)*

Librarian Jack.

**WILSON.** And then there's Carla. Carla has become a state champion in mixed martial arts – ten and under division.

*(speaks:)*

**CARLA.** Wilson! Where are your glasses?

**WILSON.** I got contacts!

**CARLA.** Looking good. Hey, don't forget: Uncle P.'s givin' us a navigation exam after recess.

**WILSON.** Oh, man!

*(She takes off.)*

**WILSON.** OK, so school can still be tough sometimes. But one thing's for sure; there's nothing to be afraid of. Except that, someday, fourth grade is going to *end*.

*(sings:)*

SOMETIMES OUR PROBLEMS SEEM SO BAD
WE THINK WE SHOULD JUST STAY HOME AND BE SAD

**UNCLE PIRATE.**

THEY MAKE US FEEL LIKE HIDING

**CAPTAIN JACK.**

THEY MAKE US FEEL AFRAID

**ALL.**

BUT WHEN YOU THINK YOU CAN'T BEAR THE LOAD
REMEMBER THE TRUSTY PIRATE CODE
IT WORKS IF YOU'RE SEVENTY FOUR
OR YOU'RE STILL IN FOURTH GRADE.
CUZ THERE'S NOTHING TO BE SCARED OF
AND WE ARE NOT AFRAID.
NO THERE'S NOTHING TO BE SCARED OF
AND WE ARE NOT AFRAID!
ARGH!

**The End.**

# OTHER TITLES AVAILABLE FROM SAMUEL FRENCH

## LITTLE GREEN MEN

### Book, Music and Lyrics by Scott Martin

*Musical Comedy / 4m, 5f, plus 2m child, 2f child / Simple Set*

"They come from several million miles away,
But they are not on vacation, they are here to stay!"

Several young campers and their adult counselors are stranded at a mountaintop wilderness retreat on the night of October 30th, 1938. When someone switches on the radio to Orson Welles' *War Of The Worlds* live broadcast, the night that panics America also becomes the night that panics Camp gitchiegoomie. Are little green men from Mars actually surrounding the mess hall, ready to make a mess of everyone inside? Can the feuding boys and girls work together to save themselves from the mysterious alien invasion? And why is that strange hairy, bug-eyed monster lurking in the bushes?

This hilarious, family-friendly musical recreates the innocent fun and slapstick humor of the wise-cracking, high-spirited film comedies of the late 1930s, complete with spooky campfires, ghostly shadows, hair-raising Halloween surprises and the scariest radio play of all time that nearly fooled the entire nation. The lively, toe-tapping original songs are fondly reminiscent of the popular scores from the golden age of the Warner Brothers and MGM film musicals with plenty of high-kicking, energetic and imaginative choreography in the unforgettable styles of Busby Berkeley, Fred Astaire and Gene Kelly.

This happiest-of-Halloween musical comedies is guaranteed fun for the entire family, from the youngest monster movie fan to the oldest senior who actually experienced that memorable night breathlessly cowered in front of the radio when the world was "invaded" by Little Green Men.

"Move over *Annie.* There's a new musical in town. Watch out, Broadway. *Little Green Men* are headed your way."
– *Culver City Observer*

SAMUELFRENCH.COM

# OTHER TITLES AVAILABLE FROM SAMUEL FRENCH

## A NUTTY NUTCRACKER CHRISTMAS

### Ralph Covert and G. Riley Mills

*Holiday Musical / 5m, 6f plus chorus*

The classic E.T.A. Hoffman tale has been brought into the Xbox age in this rockin' holiday treat from Ralph Covert of *"Ralph's World"* and Jeff Award winning playwright G. Riley Mills. *A Nutty Nutcracker Christmas* is a fun, fresh holiday spectacular for the entire family. Boasting holiday hits like "Welcome to Christmas Wood," "The Wind-Up Ballet," and crowd favorite "Let's Ruin Christmas," this rockin' contemporary adaptation follows Fritz and the Nutcracker through Christmas Wood. When trouble arises with the dastardly Mouse King, Fritz and Nutcracker must save the day, and young Fritz will learn there's more to life than just boys playing video games!

"Top 10 Holiday Show Pick!"
*– Chicago Tribune*